PENGUIN YOUNG READERS LICENSES
An Imprint of Penguin Random House LLC

Photo credits: cover: galaxy cluster: Stocktrek Images/Thinkstock, neon grid: morokey/iStock/Thinkstock; endpapers: neon grid: morokey/iStock/Thinkstock; page 1: galaxy cluster: Stocktrek Images/Thinkstock; pages 3–5: neon grid: morokey/iStock/Thinkstock; pages 12–13: lightning effect: tolokonov/iStock/Thinkstock; pages 38, 53: lightning effect: Cappan/iStock/Thinkstock; pages 42–43: triangle fade: chaluk/iStock/Thinkstock; page 47: lightning effect: tolokonov/iStock/Thinkstock; page 53: Akita portrait: Seregraff/iStock/Thinkstock; pages 54–55: Akita portrait: DevidDo/iStock/Thinkstock; page 59: confetti: radenmas/iStock/Thinkstock; page 64: cat licking: Astrod860/iStock/Thinkstock.

ISBN 9781524789930   10 9 8 7 6 5 4 3 2 1

MIGHTY MORPHIN POWER RANGERS

by Max Bisantz

Penguin Young Readers Licenses
An Imprint of Penguin Random House

THE CATMAND CENTER

Top secret headquarters for the MEOWER RANGERS

Good morning, ZZZordon.
What a low-key and relaxing day,
don't you think?

Good morning, Rangers.
It appears we have a disturbance just outside the city.

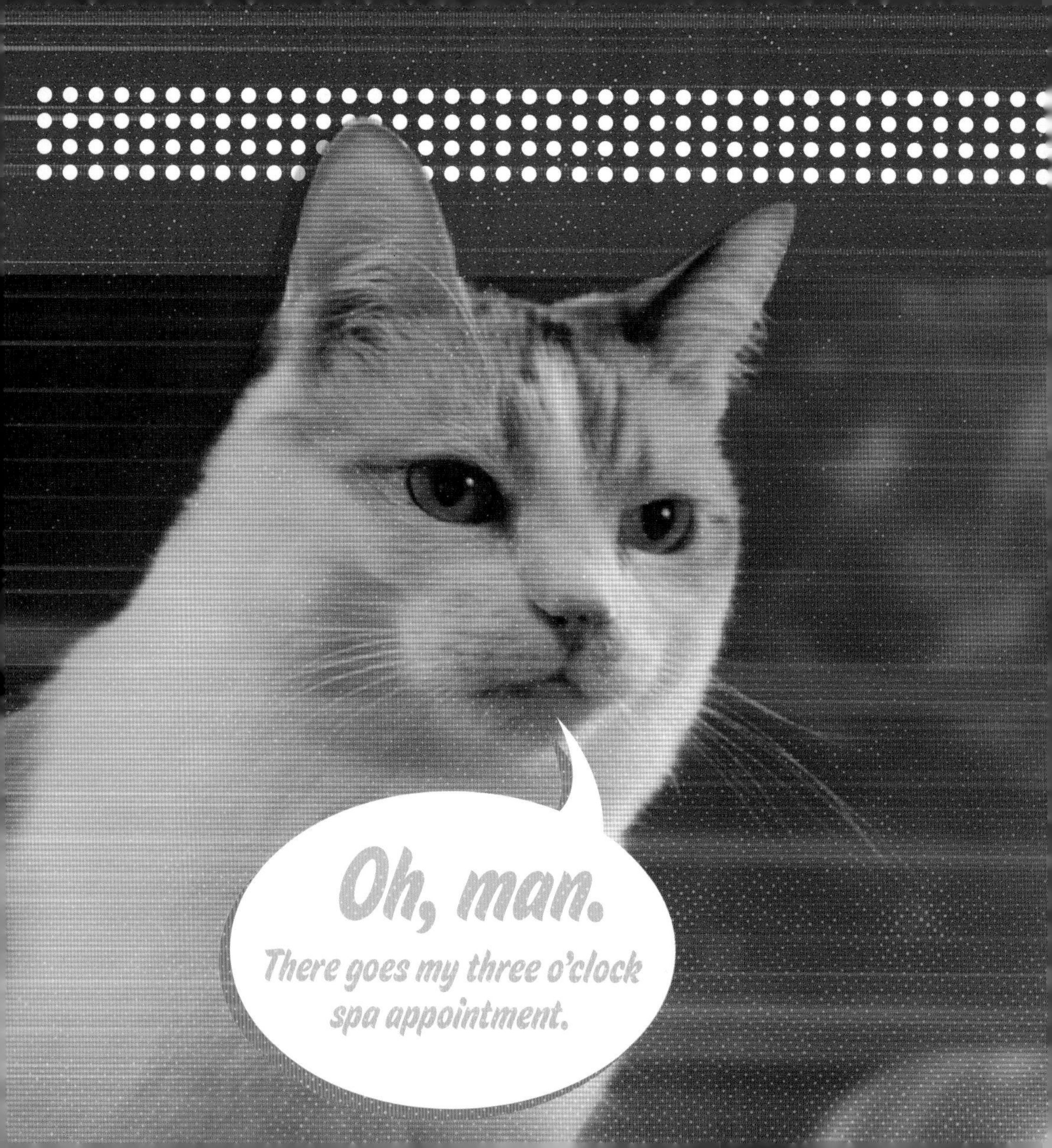
Oh, man.
There goes my three o'clock spa appointment.

Goldar Retriever has been spotted in the mountains, and Akita Repulsa is on the loose.

Suit up, Rangers. It's time for action.

IT'S
MEOWPHIN
TIME!!

DOES THIS HELMET MAKE ME LOOK FERAL?

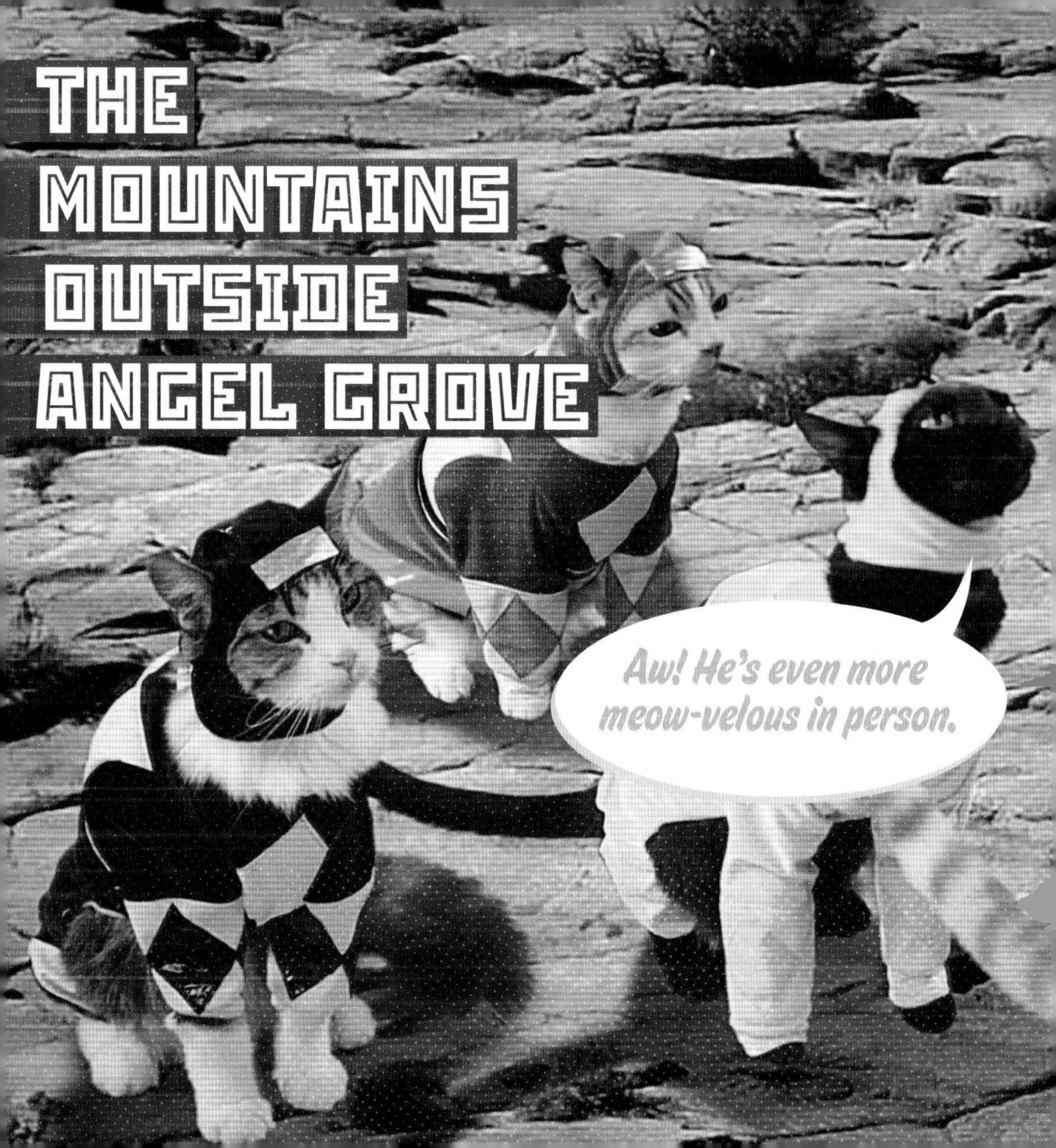
THE MOUNTAINS OUTSIDE ANGEL GROVE
Aw! He's even more meow-velous in person.

Meanwhile,

AT A SECRET LOCATION

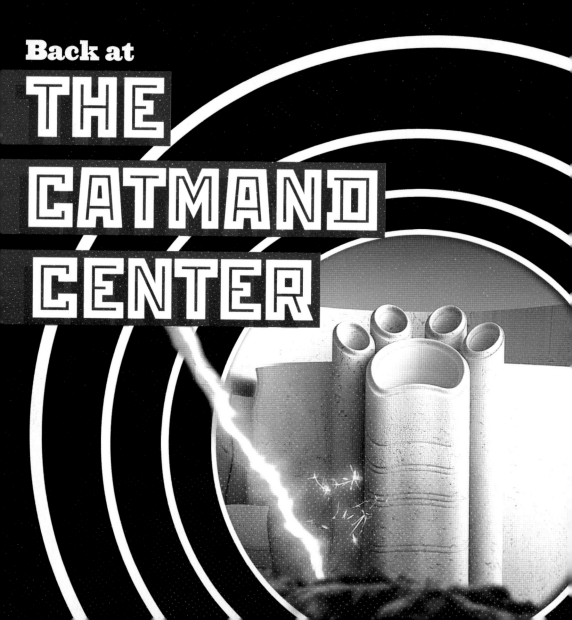

Back at

THE
CATMAND
CENTER

I AM SHOCKED.

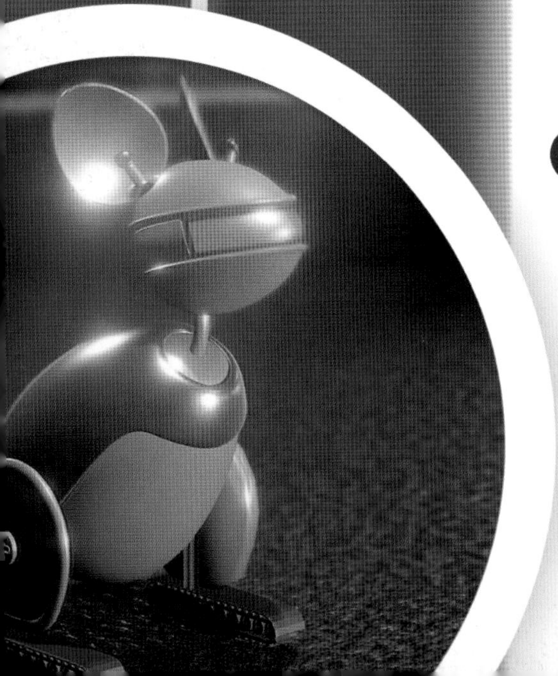

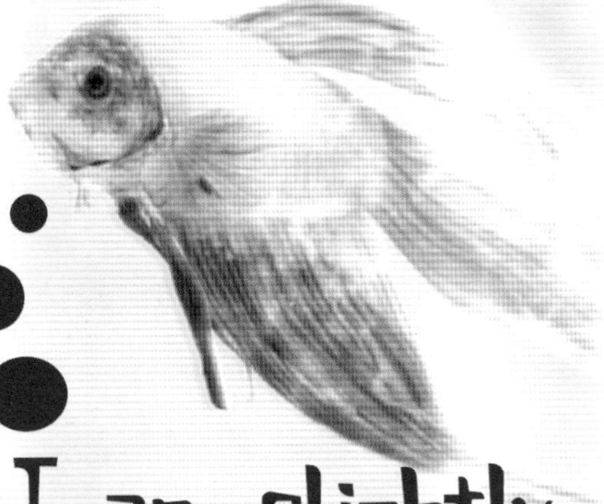

I am slightly less shocked.

Goldar Retriever has been **DEFEATED.** Now let's destroy Akita Repulsa **ONCE AND FUR ALL!**

TO THE CATMAND CENTER!

MEOWPHIN IN PROGRESS . . .

CENSORED
DUE TO
CAT ON AKITA
NASTINESS.

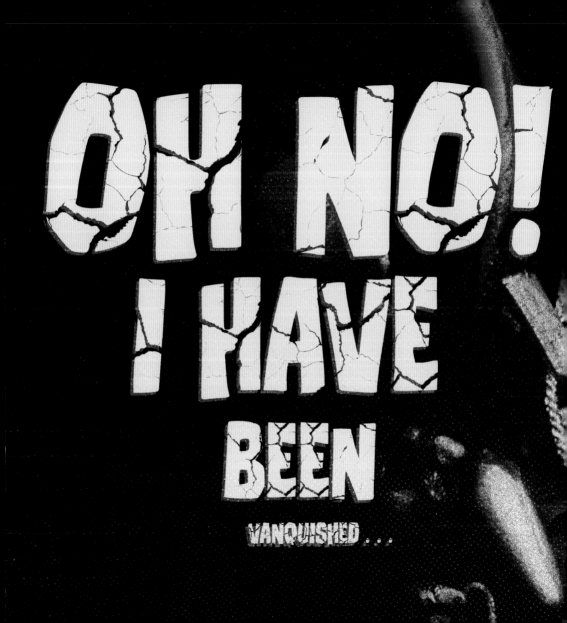

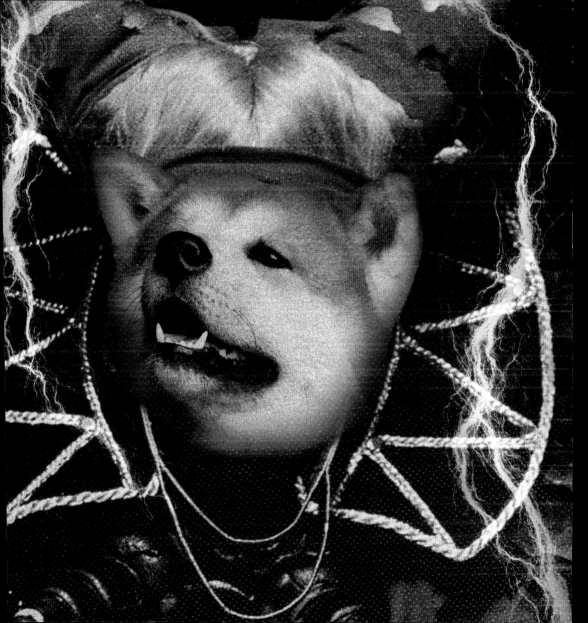

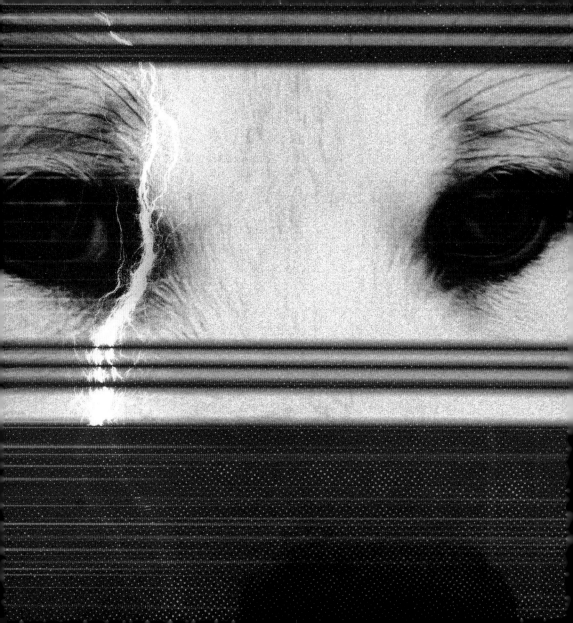

...BUT I WILL RETURN!

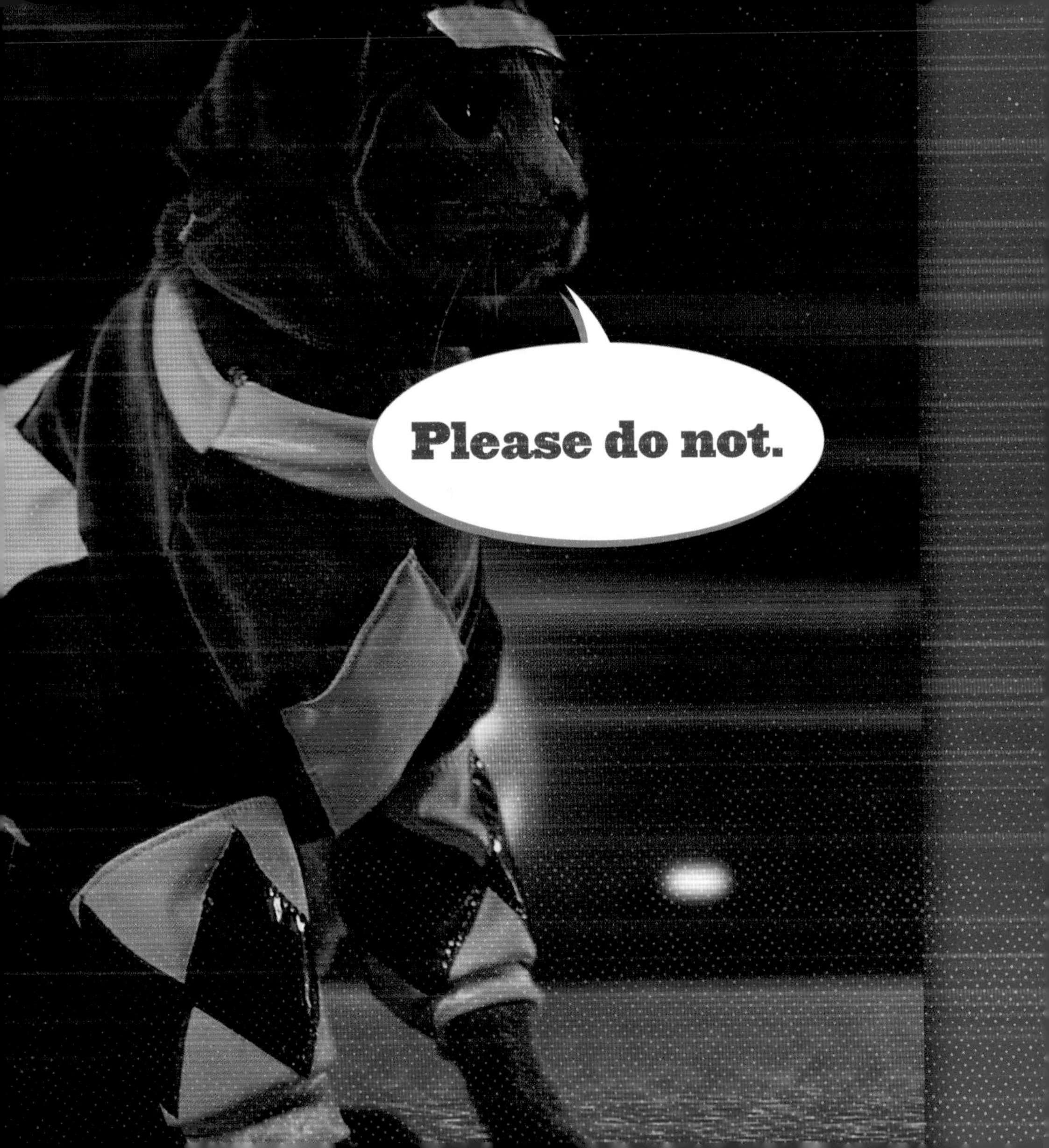
Please do not.

Congratulations, Rangers!

You have defeated the villains and protected the Meowphin Grid.

Angel Grove is once again safe.

Okay. If no one objects, I am taking off the suit.
I swear I heard someone say "tuna."